HOO. 3/04

3 1835 02395 1111

jE
Honeycutt, Natalie
Whistle home

DO NOT REMOVE
CARDS FROM POCKET

ALLEN COUNTY PUBLIC LIBRARY
FORT WAYNE, INDIANA 46802

You may return this book to any agency, branch,
or bookmobile of the Allen County Public Library.

3/94

DEMCO

P9-DTL-502

Whistle Home

story by NATALIE HONEYCUTT
pictures by ANNIE CANNON

ORCHARD BOOKS   NEW YORK

Allen County Public Library
900 Webster Street
PO Box 2270
Fort Wayne, IN 46801-2270

Text copyright © 1993 by Natalie Honeycutt
Illustrations copyright © 1993 by Annie Cannon
All rights reserved. No part of this book may be reproduced or transmitted in
any form or by any means, electronic or mechanical, including photocopying,
recording or by any information storage or retrieval system, without permission in
writing from the Publisher.

Orchard Books, 95 Madison Avenue, New York, NY 10016

Manufactured in the United States of America. Printed by Barton Press, Inc.
Bound by Horowitz/Rae. Book design by Mina Greenstein.
The text of this book is set in 15 point Plantin.
The illustrations are acrylic paintings reproduced in full color.
10 9 8 7 6 5 4 3 2 1

Library of Congress Cataloging-in-Publication Data
Honeycutt, Natalie. Whistle home / story by Natalie Honeycutt ; pictures by
Annie Cannon.   p.   cm.   "A Richard Jackson book"—Half t.p.
Summary: When Mama goes to town for the day and Dooley the dog runs off after a
rabbit, a child trusts that Aunt Whistle will be able to call them back home again.
ISBN 0-531-05490-X.   ISBN 0-531-08640-2 (lib. bdg.)
[1. Separation anxiety—Fiction.   2. Aunts—Fiction.]   I. Cannon, Annie, ill.
II. Title.   PZ7.H7467Wh   1993   [E]—dc20   92-47052

For Rod

—N.H.

AUNT WHISTLE comes up our kitchen-door path. She comes when the leaves are falling so fast you can't count them, and I'm there waiting, and so is Dooley. She comes with a sack on her shoulder that's bigger than me, but right now it's empty. Mama is leaving to drive into town.

"The apples are sweet," Mama says. "Pick lots. Only look out for worms." Then she gives a kiss to Aunt Whistle and maybe five hugs to me. And a pat to Dooley . . . but he wants to go with her!

So I hang on to Dooley, Aunt Whistle hangs on to me, and we're all tangled up when the engine goes *vroom!* and Mama is gone.

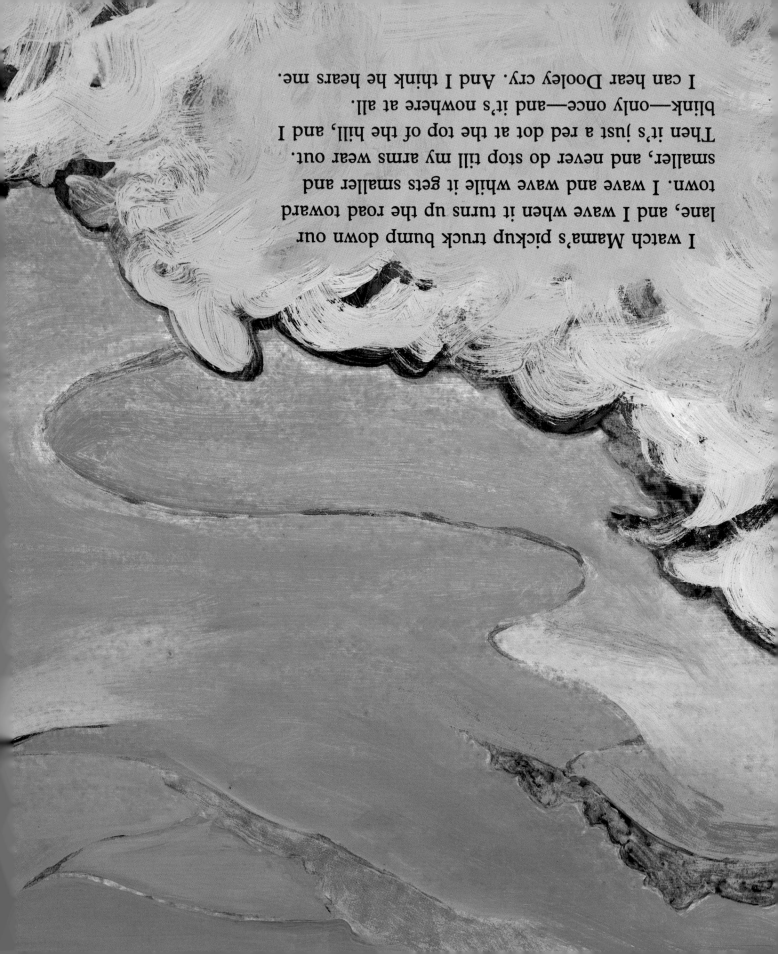

I watch Mama's pickup truck bump down our
lane, and I wave when it turns up the road toward
town. I wave and wave while it gets smaller and
smaller, and never do stop till my arms wear out.
Then it's just a red dot at the top of the hill, and I
blink—only once—and it's nowhere at all.
I can hear Dooley cry. And I think he hears me.

3 1833 02395 1111

Aunt Whistle hangs on for the longest time—that's
some hug she gives! Then at last she lets loose, and it's
time for my sweater, and holding out mittens, and now
Dooley's wagging his tail 'cause he knows: we're off to
the orchard.

Aunt Whistle walks slow and I walk fast, so we're
walking the same and she's holding my hand. But
Dooley doesn't walk—he runs, back and forth and
around us in circles, till we come to the rail fence.
We're nearly there now.

All at once, Dooley takes off with a yelp. He sticks his nose on the ground and his tail in the air. He goes zigzagging and zagging . . . then disappears—*crash!*—into the brush.

"Dooley!" I call. "Dooley, come back."

"Dooley's on the trail of a rabbit," Aunt Whistle says. "I expect he'll be home when that rabbit outruns him."

But that's too much leaving. "What if he doesn't come back?" I say. "Suppose he gets lost? Suppose he forgets about us and never comes back at all!"

"Well, then," Aunt Whistle says, "if Dooley doesn't come back on his own, I'll just whistle.

"My whistle is famous," she says. "I can whistle a groundhog right out of his burrow. I can whistle a pig from his wallow and a sheep in from clover.

"I've even whistled up skunks," she says, "though I wish that I hadn't.

"Why," she says, "I whistled your uncle Babe all the way from Kansas to marry me. If need be, I can whistle up Dooley."

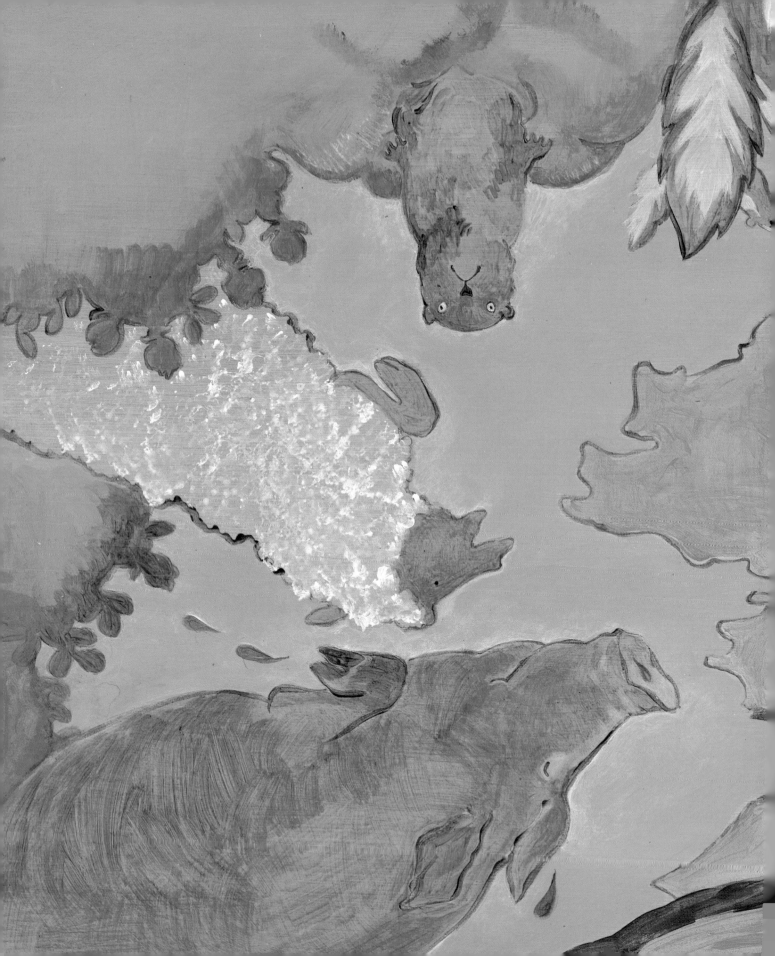

So it's me and Aunt Whistle alone in the orchard. She picks apples down from the trees, and I pick them up from the ground. I turn apples over, finding doorways for worms. It takes plenty of apples to fill up that sack, but finally we're done.

Only Dooley's still gone.

Aunt Whistle dusts her hands on her pants and says, "I expect that dog needs a whistle."

She sticks two fingers into her mouth and lets out a blast. It zooms over our valley and zooms right back, and I need to hold on to my ears! Then I wait. And I stand very still, and I'm hoping, and looking to see if that whistle will work.

When—*crash!*—here comes Dooley, running back from the brush. And I guess he can't stop, 'cause he lands flat on me!

It's a long time getting home then, with Dooley in
circles right in our way and that sack full of apples
and us stopping to rest.

And it's a longer time still
combing Dooley and pulling
those cockleburs out of his coat.
But that's what we're doing,
Aunt Whistle and me, out on the
porch steps, and I look twenty
times down to the road, or
maybe a thousand, and up to the
hilltop. And try not to blink.
But nobody's there.
"Aunt Whistle," I say, "Aunt
Whistle, I need you to whistle
again."

"Now, why's that?" she asks. "Dooley's right here, and we don't want a skunk."

"I need you to whistle up Mama," I say. "She's not coming back."

Then Aunt Whistle sets down the comb and gets me all tangled up in one of those hugs, and says,

"She *is* coming back. Yes, she is. Not right away, but soon, she'll be back. I don't *need* to whistle for her," she says. "Your mama will come back all by herself."

So we wait, there on the steps by the kitchen-door
path. And I look down our lane, and out to the road,
and not right away . . . but soon . . .

She comes back. Bringing hugs and pats and kisses
for us, and extras for me, Mama comes back.
All by herself.